THE ZACH & ZOE MYSTERIES

MYSTERIES

THE HALL OF FAME HEIST

ALSO BY #1 BESTSELLER MIKE LUPICA

Travel Team

Heat

Miracle on 49th Street

Summer Ball

The Big Field

Million-Dollar Throw

The Batboy

Hero

The Underdogs

True Legend

QB 1

Fantasy League

Fast Break

Last Man Out

Lone Stars

Shoot-Out

No Slam Dunk

Strike Zone

THE ZACH & ZOE MYSTERIES:

The Missing Baseball

The Half-Court Hero

The Football Fiasco

The Soccer Secret

The Hockey Rink Hunt

The Lacrosse Mix-Up

THE ZACH & ZOE MYSTERIES

THE HALL OF FAME HEIST

Mike Lupica

illustrated by

Chris Danger

PHILOMEL

Philomel Books
An imprint of Penguin Random House LLC, New York

Published simultaneously by Puffin Books and Philomel Books,
imprints of Penguin Random House LLC, 2020

Text copyright © 2020 by Mike Lupica
Illustrations copyright © 2020 by Chris Danger

Philomel Books is a registered trademark of Penguin Random House LLC.

Visit us online at penguinrandomhouse.com

LIBRARY OF CONGRESS CATALOGING-IN-PUBLICATION DATA IS AVAILABLE UPON REQUEST

Printed in the United States of America

ISBN: 9781984836892

1 3 5 7 9 10 8 6 4 2

Design by Maria Fazio
Text set in Fournier MT Std.

This book is for Dana Leydig,
the real best friend to Zach and Zoe.

THE ZACH & ZOE MYSTERIES

MYSTERIES

THE HALL OF FAME HEIST

ONE

Zach and Zoe were playing catch in their backyard when Zoe asked her twin brother, "What are the two greatest words in the English language?"

"That's easy," Zach said. "Ice cream."

Zoe grinned at him. They both knew how much he loved ice cream.

"We haven't even had dinner yet," Zoe said. "It's too early to be thinking about dessert."

"Ice cream isn't just dessert," Zach argued.

"If I were in charge, you'd be able to have it with every meal of the day. Including breakfast."

It was finally spring in Middletown. But the beautiful, warm day they were having made it feel like summer.

"Okay, think about two more words that are just as great," Zoe said.

"Baseball!" Zach said, before going into a big windup and firing the ball in his sister's direction.

"That's just one word, silly," Zoe said, catching the ball in her mitt. "Try again."

"Uhhh . . . snow day?" Zach said. "Two words that describe one perfect day."

Zoe reached her hands out at her sides and looked up at the clear blue sky. The trees in their backyard were blowing in the breeze.

"How can you even think about snow on a day like this?" Zoe said.

"Okay, you got me," Zach said, lifting his hands in surrender. "I can't always read your mind, you know. Why don't you just tell me the two words you're thinking of?"

Zoe wound up and threw a perfect pitch across the yard into the pocket of Zach's glove. It was the kind of throw that made Zach think his sister had the best arm of any eight-year-old in Middletown.

"Field trip," Zoe Walker said.

"Oh, yeah!" Zach Walker said. "Field trip is even better than ice cream, especially when it's a baseball field trip."

The third graders from Middletown Elementary were taking just such a field trip the next day. The National Baseball Hall of Fame and Museum in Cooperstown, New York, had recently started having small traveling museums visit towns around the country. It had begun with a few exhibits of famous photographs from baseball history. Now it was bringing more items on tour. Zach and Zoe had visited the Hall of Fame with their parents during the summer. But the museum added new items all the time. The twins were excited to explore the exhibits with their classmates.

"What sorts of things do you think they'll have there?" Zach asked Zoe.

Zoe thought back to when she and her brother visited the museum last summer. There were displays of baseballs and bats and gloves and spikes that had once belonged to the greatest baseball players who ever lived. Zoe's favorites were the uniforms of the players who had been voted into the Hall of Fame.

The Walker twins couldn't believe that Middletown had been selected to host one of the traveling museums. It had all started with a letter from their dad, Danny Walker, to the people in charge of the Hall of Fame. The museum held a contest as a way to choose which towns they'd be stopping at on their tour. So Danny Walker, with the help of his kids, decided to enter. He had to write a letter to the Hall of Fame explaining why Middletown should be chosen. In the letter, he wrote about the great Hank Aaron, who had broken Babe Ruth's all-time home run record back in the 1970s. At one time, Hank had played for a team called the Indianapolis Clowns, before he got to the major leagues.

The Clowns used to travel all over the country to play games. Early in the 1950s they had come to Middletown, which had a minor league team known as the Middletown Thunder.

Not only did Hank Aaron play a game against the Thunder at Middletown Park, he hit a home run that cleared the fences and traveled nearly all the way to the Middletown River. Because Hank Aaron went on to become a legend, that game between the Clowns and the Thunder was remembered as the most famous baseball game ever played in Middletown.

Danny Walker wrote about that game in his letter. He explained how Middletown was a small town that loved baseball just as much as its capital of Cooperstown, New York. He wrote that Middletown was a place that was also rich in baseball history.

A few months later, he received a letter back. Of over two hundred participants, Danny Walker was one of ten winners of their contest. Middletown would be a stop on the Hall of Fame museum tour. The exhibit would, of course, feature Hank Aaron. But there would also be information about other great players of his time, like Jackie Robinson. Zach and Zoe knew from their history lessons that Jackie Robinson was the first African American athlete ever to play in the major leagues. He'd paved the way for other baseball greats like Mr. Aaron.

Tomorrow, the twins and their classmates would get to see it all. Their teacher, Ms. Moriarty, and the other third grade teachers at Middletown Elementary would also be attending. A few parents were coming on the trip as well. In fact, the twins' mom, Tess Walker, had volunteered to chaperone their class. She was just as excited as Zach and Zoe to see the signed ball Hank Aaron once hit out of Middletown Park.

"The big day is almost here," Zach said to his sister. "Do you believe the museum is coming to us? It feels like they've picked up Cooperstown and set it right over Middletown."

"I know," said Zoe, bouncing on her heels. "I'm going to be too excited to sleep tonight."

"Imagine how some of those Hall of Famers felt before their games," Zach said.

Zoe nodded. "They were part of some of the biggest games in history."

"Dad says they weren't just a part of history," Zach said. "They made history."

The twins decided to take a break and go inside to read up on some of the players they would be hearing about tomorrow at Middletown's City Hall. The building would be the location for the Hall of Fame touring museum for the next week. That's why Zoe had started calling it their City Hall of Fame.

"We're going to learn so much," Zoe said. "And you know how mom always says 'knowledge is power.'"

"All I care about is getting a taste of Hank Aaron's power!" Zach said, pretending to swing an invisible baseball bat.

The old Middletown Park where the Thunder had played was long gone. It had been torn down years ago when the team left for another town. But Zach and Zoe's parents had taken them to the spot where the ballpark once stood. Then they had walked down to the river together, to where Hank Aaron's ball was said to have landed. The twins couldn't believe that somebody could have the kind of strength to hit a baseball that far.

The next morning, the twins and their classmates piled into two buses for the short ride into town. When they arrived at City Hall, they were amazed at how the entire first floor had been transformed into a baseball museum.

"It looks just like the real Hall of Fame in Cooperstown!" Zoe exclaimed.

"Except this one's only ten minutes from our house," Zach said.

Zoe's eyes wandered around the room. "How did they make it look so real?" she said.

Tess Walker put a hand on her daughter's shoulder. "When they do something at the Hall of Fame," she said, "they do it right."

The twins knew how much their mom loved baseball. She'd been a star softball pitcher at Middletown High School, and also played soccer.

"They call this a pop-up museum," Tess Walker said to the twins. "And today, baseball history is going to be popping up right before our eyes."

Zoe looked at Zach. Zach looked at Zoe. At that moment, they could read each other's minds. Today was going to be awesome.

The third graders were broken up into groups of five. Each group was assigned a tour guide and a chaperone. Naturally, Tess Walker chose to escort Zach and Zoe's group, which also included their friends Kari, Malik, and Mateo. Ms. Moriarty would be bouncing around from group to group. She wanted to be available for all her students.

Middletown's City Hall had been open for only a few months. It was brand new and beautiful inside and out. The mayor and other City Hall employees had moved their offices upstairs to make room for the baseball exhibits.

The first sign Zach and Zoe saw was the one for the Jackie Robinson exhibit. It was set up in its own room, right off the main floor. The twins couldn't wait to go inside. They had learned a lot about Jackie Robinson in school this year.

"Mr. Robinson wasn't just a great figure in baseball history," Ms. Moriarty reminded them now. "He was an important part of American history. By opening up the major league to people of color, he made baseball, and the country, better."

They saw one of Jackie Robinson's old No. 42 uniforms. None of them could believe how thick and heavy it was compared to the uniforms players wore today. They knew there was a Jackie Robinson Day every year, when players from every team wore No. 42 in Mr. Robinson's honor. Other than that, the number had been permanently retired from major league baseball.

Not all of the exhibits were about Hall of Fame players. There was one room honoring the Yankees of the 1990s, another for the Yankee team that had won four World Series in five years. There was one about the Red Sox of 2004, who'd won the first World Series for their team since 1918.

Zach and Zoe took their time in front of each display. They listened closely as their tour guide, Wendy, told them fun facts about Jackie Robinson's career. Sometimes Ms. Moriarty or Tess Walker would chip in with a fun fact of their own.

"The last player to wear No. 42 before it

was retired permanently was Mariano Rivera of the Yankees. He was the first player elected to the Hall of Fame with one hundred percent of the vote," Tess Walker told the group.

"Quit showing off, Mom," Zach whispered with a wink.

She smiled and whispered back, "Sometimes all this baseball in me just needs to get out."

With every display and exhibit, the twins were learning a lot about baseball they never knew. But they were also impatient to get to the Hank Aaron exhibit. Because he'd played in Middletown once, the twins thought of him as being *from* Middletown.

In fact, when their grandpa Richie was their age, he'd seen Hank Aaron in person when he played for the Milwaukee Braves. It was at their game against the Mets in New York that Grandpa Richie had caught Hank's home run ball. He still had it on the mantel of his fireplace.

Hank Aaron had been his favorite player ever since that day.

The twins had seen that ball plenty of times. But they'd never seen the home run ball Hank Aaron had hit in Middletown. That was about to change as Zach and Zoe's tour group entered the Hank Aaron exhibit.

Little did they know, the exhibit wasn't the only thing waiting for them inside the room. In fact, they were about to walk smack into a brand-new mystery.

Pop-up baseball museums rarely came to Zach and Zoe. But mysteries? Those seemed to follow the twins wherever they went.

TWO

The first thing they saw inside was one of Hank Aaron's old uniforms, No. 44. Like most of the items in the exhibit, it was placed behind glass to keep it safe. On the wall hung an old photo of Hank at Middletown Park the day his team played the Thunder. There were baseball bats and batting helmets. Zoe noticed a glove that looked really small compared to what outfielders wore now. Along the wall, there were lots of old photos. One showed Hank Aaron standing with Jackie Robinson. Then there were all the caps: the ones Hank Aaron wore with the Milwaukee Braves, the Atlanta Braves, even the Milwaukee Brewers, the team with which he ended his career.

Zoe said to Zach, "I really love history."

"Same," Zach said.

"More than ice cream?" she said, nudging his side.

"Yes," Zach admitted, "but don't let that get around."

"Mom says studying the past can help us understand the present," Zoe said, "and even predict the future sometimes."

"Well, I'm going to predict the future right now," said Zach. "This is definitely going to be the best field trip ever."

The Hall of Fame visitors traveled around each exhibit in an orderly way. Zach and Zoe were toward the front of the line, ahead of Kari and Malik and Mateo, going from one item to the next. The whole time, Wendy told them facts and trivia about Hank Aaron. She said his Braves teams played the Yankees twice in a seven-game World Series, each team winning one. The twins listened closely, and patiently moved along, knowing that their day was only about to get better. Because pretty soon, they'd actually get to see the one thing at City Hall they'd been most excited about: the baseball hit by Grandpa Richie's favorite player right in Middletown—the home run baseball they'd been hearing about their whole lives.

Right before they got to the table with the Aaron baseballs, Zoe and Zoe looked down and noticed a pair of latex gloves on the floor in front of them. Zoe got to them first and picked them up. Both the Walker twins were taught not to ignore litter of any kind. Luckily there was a trash can in the corner of the room, and Zoe quickly deposited the gloves there before getting back into line with Zach.

The twins finally got to the baseball table. It was protected by a large glass partition and roped off on either side. Only Hall of Fame personnel could get behind it. Malik, Mateo, and Kari came up next to the twins to gaze inside. Tess Walker and Wendy stood behind them. Ms. Moriarty had left to join another group.

The first thing they saw on the table was a large index card. It explained how Hank Aaron had played a game in Middletown once, years ago. When he hit the home run, someone retrieved the ball for him, and he held on to it for years. Then he decided to donate it to the Hall of Fame museum. The card had the date of the game on it.

There was only one small problem. Actually a big one.

When Zach and Zoe looked up from the card, they noticed the stand where the ball should have been. Except there was no ball to be found. The stand was empty.

Zach and Zoe immediately pointed this out to Wendy and their mom. For a second, Zach thought Wendy appeared to be a little nervous.

"I'm sure there's a reasonable explanation . . ." she started to say.

Zoe frowned. "Of all the baseballs here," she said to Zach, "the one we wanted to see the most is gone."

"But probably not gone for good," their mom said. "I know you both like to jump, especially when you do one of your special high fives. But let's not jump to any conclusions just yet."

Wendy, the tour guide, said she was going to get to the bottom of this. She spoke quietly into the microphone attached to her headset and walked calmly out of the room.

"I'm sure it will turn up," Tess Walker said.

"But this is the last day the museum is in town," Zach said.

It was true. Everything would be packed up after their class left the museum and driven to its next stop in Massachusetts.

"We only have a little while to explore the museum before we leave for lunch," Zoe said, "and then just one more hour in the afternoon."

"Is it possible that someone could have stolen the ball?" Mateo asked.

"It couldn't be someone from our class," Kari said. "Nobody we know would do something like that."

"I don't think so, either," Mateo said. "But where could it have gone? Everything in here is protected by glass or locked inside cases."

"Maybe our tour guide is finding out what happened to it right now," Zach said.

"It couldn't have just disappeared into thin air," Zoe said.

"If Wendy doesn't know," Zach said, "maybe we'll have to find it on our own."

"But we don't have much time," Zoe said. "If there's any hope of finding the ball, we'll have to do it before we leave."

Zach, Kari, Malik, and Mateo looked at each other. Then at Zoe again.

"If we haven't found out what happened to the ball by then," Zoe said, "it's going to feel as if it's gone for good. Who knows when we'll have another chance to see it?"

They were waiting for Wendy to come back. But like the Hank Aaron baseball, she was nowhere to be found. It was then that Zoe noticed her brother smiling at her.

"Uh-oh," he said.

"What?" she said, shrugging, even though she knew where this was going.

"You've got that look," he said.

"What look is that?" she said, knowing her excitement must be written all over her face.

"The look that says we've got a mystery to solve," Zach Walker said.

"And you've got us to help," said Malik. "We're on the same team, just like in sports."

"Everybody in Middletown always talks about how Hank Aaron hit that ball out of sight," Kari said.

"And now it's out of sight again," Zoe said. "Except it's not as simple as chasing down a home run ball."

She was worried. So was her brother. They all were. But Zach and Zoe were determined to find out what happened.

In a place full of history, the Walker twins knew they had some history of their own going for them: a history of solving mysteries just like this one. They'd dealt with a baseball mystery before, when Zach's signed ball had gone missing in their classroom.

Zoe reminded her brother of that now.

"This time we're dealing with a baseball

with even more value," she said. "Because it has Hank Aaron's signature on it."

"So it's a history mystery!" Zach said.

"Look at you," his sister said. "You sound like a poet."

"No," he said, "I'm a detective. And so are you."

They high-fived each other.

They'd talked about how coming to the museum today felt like a big game.

Now the game was on.

THREE

There were security guards posted at the door to each exhibit room. The man at the door to the Hank Aaron room was named Tony. The Walker twins knew him because he was a retired Middletown policeman who also loved baseball. He'd umpired a lot of their Little League games. They were certain it was Tony's love of baseball that made him want to volunteer at the museum this week.

Zach wasn't surprised to see Zoe walk right up to Tony. They were both detectives, but his sister didn't shy away from taking the lead. And Zach was just fine with that.

Tony's last name was McGuire, but he'd always insisted the twins call him Tony.

"Hey, Tony," Zoe said now. Zach was right there with her, eager to hear what Tony might know about the missing baseball.

"Hey yourself," he said. "How are you two enjoying the tour?"

"I'd be enjoying it a lot more if one of the baseballs hadn't gone missing," Zoe said.

"I heard something about that in my earpiece," he said. "But I'm thinking that maybe it just got misplaced."

"You mean it ended up somewhere else in the museum?" Zoe said. "Don't you think it would be a little odd for a Hank Aaron ball to show up in, say, the Ken Griffey Jr. room?" She grinned to show she was joking.

Tony chuckled. "I'd look into it myself, but I'm not supposed to leave my post."

"When you got here this morning,"

Zach said, "you didn't notice anything—or anybody—out of the ordinary, did you?"

"Just business as usual," Tony said. "The same volunteers and Hall of Fame personnel walking in and out of the exhibit rooms."

Just then, Wendy came back into the room. When Tess Walker asked if everything was all right, Wendy smiled nervously and said that she'd had better mornings. But before she could say another word, she heard something in her earpiece.

"I'm on my way," she replied. Then, to the tour group, she said, "Sorry, everyone. I've got to go handle some museum business, but you're in good hands with Tess Walker. She knows as much about baseball as any of the guides." Then, before Zach and Zoe could ask her anything about the missing baseball, she was out the door and gone.

Right then, Ms. Moriarty announced that their tour would continue with a film being shown in another room. It was a documentary about the most famous home runs in baseball history. Zach and Zoe went along with everybody else. But right now, they didn't much care about other home runs. They were only interested in the home run hit by Hank Aaron. And the ball that flew out of sight.

As they entered the screening room where they'd watch the movie, another security guard stood talking into her headset.

"What about Item 42-F?" she said. "Did that get put back in its place?"

They saw the guard smile and nod. "Yes, Marv, I know whose number that was," she said.

Zach and Zoe's eyes went wide. "Jackie Robinson," they whispered to each other at the same time.

As they filed into the room, the twins were getting farther from the guard. But they were just able to make out what she said next: "Make sure that Joey logged it in. You know the rules: You touch it, you log it."

The twins looked at each other, thinking they might have found their first clue.

"She said item 42-F," Zoe said to her brother. "So that must mean every item in the museum has a number and letter combination assigned to it."

Zach nodded. "That sounds right. After all, how else would a museum with so many items keep track of everything?"

"Exactly," Zoe said. "And she mentioned something about logging it in. . . ."

"That must be how they make sure everything's accounted for," said Zach. "Like how Ms. Moriarty takes attendance every morning. She submits the sheet to the principal's office so they know if everyone's where they should be."

Zoe thought hard about what all of this could mean. If every item had a code number, then the Hank Aaron ball must have one, too. And that meant one of the museum staff would have had to log it in at some point.

"I'm not sure how seeing the log sheet would

help us, though," Zach said. "The ball may have disappeared after it was logged in this morning."

"You're right," Zoe said as they took their seats. "But I've got a hunch it means something."

"I've learned to trust your hunches," Zach said to his sister. "But you know what I'd really like to do after this movie? Put something in my stomach."

"Are you ever not hungry?" Zoe said, teasing.

"Only when I'm sleeping," he said. "But I can't lie: most of the time, I even dream about food."

"Well," Zoe said, "I'm hungry to solve the mystery of the home run ball."

"But after lunch, please."

His sister couldn't help it. As anxious as she was about the missing ball, she laughed. Her brother could always make her laugh.

FOUR

The parent chaperones had prepared boxed lunches for all the third graders. They wanted to make the day feel like an adventure.

It was another beautiful day in Middletown, so the buses drove them all to Wesley Park for lunch. Everyone sat at long picnic tables and talked about what they'd seen so far. They would still have time after lunch to explore the rooms and exhibits they hadn't visited already.

"Baseball was never my favorite sport," Kari

said. "But I like it a lot more after everything we learned this morning."

"That's what history does," Ms. Moriarty said. "The more you know about something, the more you appreciate it. And if it's really interesting, you'll want to research it on your own."

"My favorite part," Kari said, "was how brave Jackie Robinson was, being the first person of color to get to play in the major leagues."

"It shouldn't have taken as long as it did," Ms. Moriarty said. "But because of his talent and the grace he showed under great pressure, he made it easier for other African American players like Hank Aaron who came after him."

"By then," Tess Walker said, "baseball really was America's national pastime. Because the sport was open to anyone good enough to play in the majors, no matter the color of their skin."

Hearing about Jackie Robinson made Zach and Zoe realize that great athletes of the past didn't just change sports, they changed the country for the better.

Everyone continued eating their lunches and chatting about the museum. But Zoe couldn't help but think about Hank Aaron's missing baseball. She would have been happy to keep searching right through their lunch break, but she knew she had to stay with their class.

When they'd all finished eating, they deposited their boxes in the recycling bin and threw any other trash away, just as Zoe had done with the latex glove she'd found on the floor. Her classmates knew it was wrong to litter.

But now, Zoe's focus was totally back on the missing ball.

"It makes no sense," she said. "Why would they put out the index card and the ball stand without the ball on it?"

"Maybe different people were in charge of different items," Zach offered, "and someone forgot to bring the ball."

"But Wendy, our tour guide, seemed upset," Zoe said. "She didn't give us any update on the ball when she came back to the Hank Aaron room."

"So you think it was there and then it wasn't?" Zach said.

"That's exactly what I'm saying," Zoe said. "And I've got a feeling it has something to do with what we heard that guard say earlier."

"About logging in items?" Zach said.

"Yep. I just don't know exactly how."

Ms. Moriarty came over to the twins then, and told them there were still twenty minutes left before they had to head back to City Hall. She smiled and said, "Any thoughts on how we could spend that time?"

Zach and Zoe looked at each other, knowing they were reading each other's minds, as usual.

"What about a baseball game!" they said at the same time.

"Well," Ms. Moriarty said, "as a matter of fact, I happen to have a Wiffle Ball and bat that would be perfect for this occasion. They're on the bus. Why don't I grab them while you two get everyone together?"

Because it was a weekday afternoon, the field at Wesley Park wasn't being used. The field was in tip-top shape for the beginning of Little League season in Middletown: freshly mown green grass, crisp painted white lines. Even the dirt in the infield and around home plate looked new.

"That field is practically begging us to have a game," Zach said.

It turned out they had time for two fast innings. Zach pitched for one team, while Zoe pitched for the other. Ms. Moriarty had brought one of the larger-sized Wiffle Balls. It was almost as big as a softball, making it easier to hit. Nobody could hit it very far, but everybody was making solid contact and getting the ball into the air. It was a breezy day, so part of the fun was chasing the fly balls around as if they were Frisbees.

A pickup lunchtime game like this reminded the twins of the way sports could bring people together. It could make them feel as if they were one team, even when they were competing against each other.

The score was tied in the bottom of the second, with two outs and the bases loaded, when Zach came to the plate to face his sister.

"Who are you pretending to be?" Zoe called in from the mound.

"Hank Aaron, of course!" Zach said.

"Think you can hit it over the fence?" she called.

"No way," Zach said. "Doesn't mean I won't try."

She threw him a perfect pitch, and Zach connected, hitting the ball on a line over Malik's head and into the outfield. It soared as far as anybody had hit one that afternoon, and it was enough to send Mateo all the way home, winning the game for their team.

When Malik brought the ball back in from the outfield, he handed it to Ms. Moriarty, who grinned and said, "Do you think we should have Zach autograph the ball?"

They all laughed. It had been a good game, but now Zach and Zoe knew it was time to get back to work. There was a real autographed ball out there that was missing. Out of sight, but not out of mind. At least not for the Walker twins.

FIVE

When they got back to City Hall, Kari, Malik, Mateo, and the twins were brought inside a conference room. But for this week, it had been turned into what looked like the most awesome jewelry store in the world.

Because there, under a glass counter, were World Series rings. Some went as far back as the 1940s and 1950s. Others were from more recent years, like the one the Red Sox had gotten after they won the 2018 World Series against the Dodgers.

Zach and Zoe and their friends walked slowly past the rings. It was as if they were glowing inside the case. The woman behind the counter, Mrs. Keith, who worked for the real Hall of Fame in Cooperstown, explained some of the designs to them. She pointed out something the kids could see plainly enough for themselves.

With each year, the rings seemed to grow larger in size, with more diamonds and gemstones in each design.

"Some of them look as big as baseballs," Zach whispered to his sister.

"If somebody tossed me one," Zoe said, "I think I'd need my glove to catch it."

Just then the woman from the Hall of Fame asked if anybody in the room would like to hold the Red Sox World Series ring.

Everybody's hand shot up at once. Zach's was one of them, of course. He tried to act calm and not overly excited. He loved the Red Sox and Fenway Park. His parents would sometimes take him and his sister on road trips to Boston just to see a game.

Zach thought maybe, just maybe, the woman from the Hall of Fame would be like Zoe in that moment and read his mind. As luck would have it, she smiled and pointed right at him.

Zach suddenly felt as nervous as if he were standing at the plate in a real baseball game, with the winning run at third base.

He put out both his hands squeezed together at the sides across the glass counter. Thankfully, they weren't shaking, even though he was afraid he might drop the ring as soon as it was given to him.

"Not just yet," Mrs. Keith said to Zach. "First we have to put these on."

She pulled out a box of latex gloves from the shelf behind her. Then she handed Zach a pair while she put on her own.

Zach couldn't help but notice that these gloves looked exactly like the ones he and Zoe had spotted that morning. The ones on the floor of the Hank Aaron exhibit.

He eyed Zoe from across the room and knew she was thinking the same thing.

Zach took the gloves from Mrs. Keith and put them on carefully. As he did, he could see Zoe staring at him, wide-eyed.

"We always wear gloves when handling precious items like these," Mrs. Keith said. "Our job in Cooperstown isn't just to celebrate the history of our game. It's to preserve it for future generations like yours."

Then Mrs. Keith turned a key in the lock of the glass case and removed the ring carefully. She came around from behind the counter and approached Zach.

"Ready?" she said.

"Ready," he said, breathing hard. This was a special moment, and Zach was taking it all in.

She placed the ring gently in the palm of his right hand.

"Whoa," Zach said. He couldn't believe how heavy it was. The diamonds sparkled in the light of the room.

In that moment, it was as if Zach were holding the whole World Series in the palm of his hand.

As soon as he handed the ring back to Mrs. Keith and took off his gloves, Zach gave a quick low five to his sister.

"Mrs. Keith just handed you a huge World Series ring," Zoe said to him, keeping her voice low. "But she also handed both of us a huge clue."

"I knew those gloves looked familiar," Zach said. "You're thinking what I'm thinking, right?"

Zoe grinned and nodded. "Those weren't just any gloves we found on the floor," she said. "They're a clue to the mystery, for sure."

Then she gave her brother another low five. They had seen so many valuable items today, including famous baseball gloves.

But the only glove they cared about now was one made out of latex.

SIX

As soon as they were out on the main floor again, Zoe Walker could no longer contain herself.

"I should have known those gloves we found on the floor were another clue!" she blurted to Zach.

"But we didn't even know the ball was missing yet," Zach said, trying to make her feel better.

"I still should have picked up on it," Zoe said. "Everything else is so neat and organized at our City Hall of Fame. And those gloves looked out of place just sitting there by themselves on the floor. Once we discovered the ball was missing, I should have done what Mom always says: connect the dots."

"Come on," Zach said. "No one is better at connecting dots than you are. Let's focus on the positives. We've got another clue."

Their group was now moving in the direction of the Ken Griffey Jr. exhibit, led by Tess Walker. There was only a short time left of their field trip, and they assumed Wendy wouldn't be returning to their group. Zoe still thought that was suspicious, but they had real clues now. That might be enough to solve the mystery on their own.

Zach and Zoe hung near the back, so they could compare notes.

And connect dots.

"Whoever took the Hank Aaron ball out of the case must have been wearing gloves," Zoe said. "Obviously they didn't drop the ball. But they did drop some gloves."

Zach grinned and poked his sister with a playful elbow.

"When we find out who it was," he said, "we're definitely going to have to charge that person with an error."

Zoe looked at her brother and shook her head.

"Come on," he said. "Admit that was funny."

"I'll admit it was clever," Zoe said. "But it won't be funny if we don't solve this mystery before we leave City Hall."

Up ahead of them, Malik and Mateo were talking about Ken Griffey Jr. They'd been reading up on him in anticipation of the field trip.

Malik reminded Mateo that before Mariano Rivera was elected with 100 percent of the vote, it was Ken Griffey Jr. who'd had the highest percentage, over 98 percent.

"He was before our time, too," Malik said.

Mateo smiled and said, "Just a lot closer to our time!"

Behind them Zach and Zoe were still fixated on the latex gloves.

"What this has to mean," Zoe said to her brother, "is that whoever took the ball out of its holder works here. Nothing else makes sense. Mom didn't bring gloves with her. Neither did Ms. Moriarty, or any of us."

"That's probably why Tony said he hadn't seen anything—or anybody—unusual," Zach said.

"But that doesn't mean something unusual didn't go on," Zoe said. "Or our tour guide wouldn't have been so upset before. You saw her face when we pointed out that the Hank Aaron ball wasn't where it was supposed to be. She looked worried."

"We haven't even seen Wendy since we got back from lunch," Zach said.

Ms. Moriarty was back now to join their group. She stood inside the exhibit room, in front of a locker that had Ken Griffey Jr.'s No. 24 uniform hanging inside. Then she called out to the Walker twins.

"I hope you two are talking baseball," she said.

Zach looked at his sister and grinned.

"We are talking baseball," he said.

He just didn't tell his teacher that they were only talking about one specific baseball at the moment.

SEVEN

The last stop on their tour was the gift shop, which took up a big space in the front lobby of their very own Hall of Fame. They staggered the tour groups so that the gift shop wouldn't become too crowded. Now it was Zach and Zoe's group's turn in the store.

And as much as Zach and Zoe wanted to keep searching for the Hank Aaron ball, they knew it was important to stay with their group. They were part of a team, like in sports. And that was just as special as competing.

And solving mysteries.

But they knew they were running out of time. Once they got back on the buses for the trip back to Middletown Elementary, they might not ever see the Hank Aaron ball with their own eyes. Worse for Zach and Zoe, they might never find out what happened to it.

Their father, Danny Walker, had always told the twins that part of what he loved most about baseball was that it was really the only team sport without a clock.

But now Zach and Zoe knew they were on the clock.

There were all sorts of cool items in the gift shop, key chains and posters and Hall of Fame caps and even T-shirts. Looking around, Zach and Zoe once again felt as if they had made another trip to Cooperstown, and not just a short ride into their own town. Tess Walker had given each of them an early allowance to use in the shop.

Zach decided to use his money to buy a pack of Hall of Fame baseball cards. Zoe picked out a Red Sox key chain. The Sox were her favorite team, too, though, she didn't follow them as closely or as passionately as her brother did.

When they got up to the cash register, the twins looked up and saw a name tag first. It was pinned to the shirt of the young man standing behind the counter. But Zach and Zoe noticed the name.

The name tag read Joey.

"Wait," Zoe said. "You're Joey!"

"For my whole life," the boy said, smiling. "And who are you two?"

The twins introduced themselves.

"Walker," Joey said. "You wouldn't happen to be related to Danny Walker, would you?"

The twins nodded. They got this all the time. "Danny Walker is our dad," Zach told him.

"Wow! Everyone in Middletown knows

Danny Walker. I watch him on TV all the time," Joey said.

Danny Walker had once been a star basketball player in the NBA. But everyone knew him now as the sports broadcaster he was today.

Zoe told Joey they were here on a field trip with their class.

"You must have learned a lot today," Joey said as he rang them up.

"Just not as much as we'd like to have learned," Zoe said.

"Is there any way I can help?" Joey said. "I love baseball and feel like I know a lot about it. I'm even the starting shortstop on the Middletown High team this year. It's why I volunteered to work this week at the museum."

Malik, Mateo, and Kari were still shopping, so for now Zach and Zoe were the only ones at the register.

Zoe asked Joey if they could ask him a few questions.

Joey must have thought she meant baseball questions, because he said, "Of course! I actually know a lot of baseball history. In fact, I'd been hoping they might let me be a tour guide this week."

"Well," Zoe said, "we heard one of the security guards mention someone named Joey a little while ago. It sounded like it had to do with logging in items from the exhibits."

"Would you know anything about that?" Zach asked.

"I might," Joey said. "I haven't only worked in the gift shop this week. That was just my job for the last day. I've had a bunch of different jobs. Early this morning my job was to go through some of the exhibit rooms. I had to make sure the items looked good as new, even if this was the Hall's last day here."

"Does that mean all the items?" Zoe said.

"No," Joey said. "Some of those uniforms and spikes and gloves are supposed to look old.

But today they let me polish up the World Series rings. It was fun, even though when I finished, I had to log in that I'd handled them all."

Zoe looked at Zach, almost knowing he was reading her mind. He nodded, because they both knew the question Zoe needed to ask next.

"Did you happen to handle any baseballs today?" Zoe said.

Just like that, Joey was the one who looked nervous, as if he were at the plate in a pressure situation.

"Well . . . wait, yes . . . but why do you ask?" he said.

Now his cheeks were pink, and he looked around anxiously.

"Actually," Zach said, "we just wanted to ask you about one baseball in particular."

Joey leaned across the counter so only the twins could hear what he said next.

"Are you talking about the Hank Aaron

ball?" he said, almost whispering.

Both the Walker twins nodded.

Joey took a deep breath, then let it out. He almost sounded relieved.

"How did you know?" he asked.

EIGHT

"It just happens to be the one item we wanted to see the most," Zoe said.

"And we think there may have been some kind of mistake," Zach said. "Because it wasn't there when it was supposed to be our turn to see it."

They were keeping their own voices as low as possible.

"We've been hearing about that ball our whole lives, because he hit the home run right here in Middletown," Zoe said. "And because

Mr. Aaron is our grandfather's favorite player."

"Now we're just trying to figure out what happened to it," Zach said.

"The thing is," Zoe said, "we didn't come here today looking for a mystery. But one seems to have found us anyway,"

Joey gulped. He seemed to be thinking hard about something.

"Did you see the ball this morning?" Zoe asked.

"Yes . . ." Joey said, quietly.

Then he told them how when he'd arrived at work that morning, he found out one of the rooms he was scheduled to clean was the one with the Aaron exhibit in it.

"I'm the same as the two of you," he said, "even though I'm obviously a little older. I've been hearing about that home run all my life. It was the first thing I went to see the day the museum opened. But when I got here today, it was as if it had been neglected since then. Its holder was all dusty. And there was enough dust on the ball that even Mr. Aaron's autograph was hard to see."

"So did you clean it off?" Zach said.

"We're not supposed to clean it ourselves," Joey explained. "There are professionals who do that. I'm only supposed to identify the items that need cleaning or dusting."

Zach and Zoe listened closely. They knew they were close to solving the mystery.

"So I carefully took the ball out of its case,

and put it back into the small box it came in," he said. "I thought I'd leave it for the Hall of Fame employees to take care of. I meant to tell them. But I guess I forgot."

"Where did you put the box?" Zoe asked.

"Right behind the table," Joey said. "Where it would be safe and secure."

"Did you log it out?" Zach said.

"I . . . I think I did," Joey said.

Then he paused, and closed his eyes, as if he were trying to watch a replay of what he'd done inside his own head.

But when he opened them again, he was shaking his head from side to side.

"Oh no," he said. "No, no, no."

"So then you don't know that everyone is looking for it now?" Zach asked.

"We just assumed everybody's been talking about it on their headsets," Zoe said.

Joey said he wasn't wearing one today because his main job was working in the gift shop. "You mean nobody saw the box behind the table?" Joey said, a look of alarm on his face.

"Nope," Zoe said.

"I knew something was going on," Joey said, "but I didn't know what. I've been stationed here at the gift shop since then. I know that your class went to lunch, but there's been a steady crowd of people in here the whole day."

"Well, we can tell you what's been going on," Zach said.

"A Hall of Fame mystery," his sister said, finishing the thought.

NINE

Joey told the twins he was afraid he was going to get in trouble with his baseball coach at Middletown High. The coach was the one who'd encouraged him to volunteer for this job. Joey was also concerned that everyone who worked for the Hall of Fame would remember the way he'd messed up with the Hank Aaron ball. He didn't want to disappoint them or make them think they'd made a mistake hiring him for the job.

Zach and Zoe told him not to worry, they were sure everything was going to work out fine. Even though they were only eight, and Joey was a teenager, they helped calm him down.

"We don't just solve mysteries," Zach said.

"Sometimes we solve problems, too," Zoe said.

"And if we can't solve them, there's somebody here who might be the best problem-solver in the world," Zach said.

"Who's that?" Joey asked.

"Our mom!" the twins said together.

Tess Walker was talking to Ms. Moriarty outside the shop. They were planning to take the kids to see one last bonus exhibit. One that showed some of the greatest game endings in World Series history.

The twins apologized for interrupting, but told their mom and teacher they had something important to tell them. Then they took turns telling the story of the missing ball and the part Joey had played in it. They spoke fast, the words pouring out of them. Zach and Zoe finished each other's sentences the way they often did. They explained about the latex gloves and hearing Joey's name, and the part about logging in items.

They were both out of breath by the time they'd finished.

"Anyway," Zoe said, "that's how we think the ball went missing in the first place."

Ms. Moriarty smiled at Tess Walker.

"Once again, they're both A students when it comes to solving mysteries," Ms. Moriarty said.

"*A* for Aaron!" Zach cheered.

They all headed to the Hank Aaron exhibit now, where they found Tony still at his post. Tess Walker asked if he could call Wendy through his headset and tell her to meet them at the gift shop.

"What's going on?" Tony asked.

Zach and Zoe grinned.

"Sometimes a baseball is remembered because one of the greatest players of all time nearly hits it into the Middletown River," Zach said.

"Now we're going to remember that same ball after it only traveled a few feet," Zoe said.

"Not sure I understand . . ." Tony said.

"Don't worry," Zoe said, "you will pretty soon."

They all met Wendy in the gift shop, and Joey explained to her what had happened. He said he was only trying to do the right thing, but the result came out all wrong. And that he'd understand if he lost his job, even though the job ended that day anyway.

"Well, that's not going to happen," Wendy said. "You've been one of our best workers all week. But you do understand that none of this drama would have happened if you'd simply logged the ball out, or told someone where it was."

Joey hung his head.

"I feel like I struck out on my last at-bat," he said.

"Don't worry," she said. "Luckily for you, the Walker twins came up right after you and hit home runs."

"The way Hank Aaron always did," Tony said. "Seven hundred and fifty-five for his career."

"But you know what?" Tess Walker said. "Even though he hit that many home runs, he struck out nearly twice as much. But he kept swinging. It's the same in life. Sometimes the most valuable lessons are learned from our mistakes."

"I've sure learned mine," Joey said. "I never want to make that kind of mistake again."

"I'm sure you won't," Wendy said, and winked at Joey. "Now, let's go find that ball!"

Joey found someone to cover for him at

the gift shop and they followed Wendy to the Hank Aaron exhibit. Once inside the room, Wendy let herself in behind the table of baseballs and reached for a clean pair of gloves. Zach and Zoe peered knowingly at each other. Everything was coming full circle. The same kind of gloves that were used to remove the ball were now being used to retrieve it. Wendy bent down behind the table and came back up holding a baseball in her hand. *The* baseball. The one Hank Aaron hit right out of Middletown Park.

"Whoa," Zach and Zoe said at once. They couldn't tear their eyes away. At that moment, it was as if they'd forgotten all about solving the mystery. Right now, they could only focus on the ball in front of them. All that history in one small package. Kari, Malik, and Mateo came up beside the twins to gaze at the ball in Wendy's hand.

"It was worth the wait," Zach finally said.

Zoe nodded in agreement.

Once everyone had had enough time to look at the ball, Wendy placed it back on its stand on the table.

Then Zoe turned to Joey. "You know what the best part of today was?" she said "Even though we lost that ball for a little while, we all learned a whole lot. Not just about baseball, but about museum management!"

Everyone laughed. "And I think we all learned something else," Joey said. "Along with great baseball players, Middletown also has some pretty great detectives!"

Then Zach explained to Joey that when he and his sister solved a mystery or did something memorable in sports there was a way they liked to celebrate.

At that moment, the Walker twins did their special high five. They spun around and jumped and bumped elbows and hips the way they always did, while everyone cheered them on.

Joey looked at the twins and said, "Well, there's only one way to describe what I just saw."

They all waited.

"Hall of Fame moves!"

TEN

As a way of thanking Zach and Zoe for helping the Hall of Fame find the missing ball, Wendy offered each of the twins a gift of their choice from the souvenir shop.

The twins briefly consulted with each other, then told Wendy one gift would do for the two of them:

A signed Hank Aaron baseball card.

"But whose room is it going in?" Tess Walker said.

Zach looked at Zoe, and said, "Neither of ours."

It had been part of their private conversation.

"We'll explain later," he told their mom.

Tess turned to Wendy and said, "Even after the mysteries are over, my children love to be mysterious."

"But we will give you a hint," Zoe said. "Aren't you always telling us that history is something we're supposed to pass on?"

"Yep," Tess Walker said. "Even if you're just passing on memories."

"Well, that's your clue," Zach said.

When they got home that afternoon, Danny Walker was waiting for them at the kitchen table. He'd come home early from work and told his kids he wanted to know everything about their day at the Hall of Fame.

Zach and Zoe grinned at each other, then at their dad.

"Best," Zoe started.

"Field trip," Zach said.

"Ever!" they shouted together.

Grandpa Richie and the twins' cousin Anthony came over for dinner that night. Zach and Zoe were more than happy to tell them, and their dad, about the mystery of the missing ball. Danny Walker always said that the best conversation he heard all day was at their own kitchen table. And tonight was no exception.

"I know you've all heard me say this before," Grandpa Richie said, "but my all-time favorite sports hero was Hank Aaron."

"Because he hit all those home runs?" Zach asked.

"Because he hit all those home runs and was as great a gentleman as any sport has ever known," Grandpa Richie said.

When dinner was over, there was still plenty of daylight left. The twins decided that the best way to end an already perfect baseball day was another game of Wiffle Ball. This time in their own backyard. The twins and Cousin Anthony against their parents and Grandpa Richie.

Cousin Anthony flipped a coin, and Grandpa Richie called heads. Heads it was. His team would be the home team, meaning it would bat last.

The score was 3–3 when Grandpa Richie's team got last ups. Tess Walker was on third. Danny was on second. There were two outs, and Zach was pitching.

"No batter!" Zoe called out from behind Zach, smiling in at her grandfather.

"Ha!" Grandpa Richie said. "Just wait and see."

He took his stance, the Wiffle bat pointing at the sky and very still.

"The great Mr. Aaron," Grandpa Richie said, "sometimes only had to flick those strong wrists to hit balls out of sight."

That's exactly what he tried to do now on

the first pitch Zach threw him. He made perfect contact with an upper-cut home run swing even though it was a plastic bat and ball. The ball soared over Zoe's head as her mom ran home, scoring the winning run.

"Flick of the wrists just like that," Grandpa Richie said. Then he tried to do his version of the twins' celebration with Danny and Tess Walker.

They were so busy that none of them noticed when Zoe disappeared into the house.

When she came back out, she was holding something behind her back.

"I have something for the MVP of tonight's backyard game," she said. "Actually, my brother and I both do."

Then she and Zach presented Grandpa Richie with the signed Hank Aaron card that Wendy had given them in the gift shop. They were passing on one small piece of history to their grandfather, knowing how important it was to him.

Grandpa Richie looked at the card, then at the twins. His eyes got a little teary, and then he leaned down to hug them both. He told them he was going to buy a frame for the card first thing tomorrow, so it could go right next to the Hank Aaron ball on his mantel.

"Wow," Tess Walker said. "This really did turn into the perfect ending to a perfect day."

"Now what can we all do to celebrate?" Grandpa Richie said.

"I have two words for you that might not be the best in the English language," Zach said, looking at his sister, "but are close enough."

"Which two are those?" his grandfather said.

"Ice cream!"

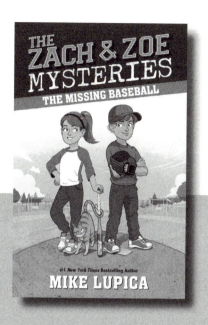

There's nothing eight-year-old twins Zach and Zoe Walker love more than playing sports and solving mysteries. And when those two worlds collide . . . well, it doesn't get any better than that. So when a baseball signed by Zach's favorite major league player suddenly goes missing—the search is on! Luckily, amateur sleuths Zach and Zoe are on the case. Can they solve the mystery and find the ball before it's lost for good?

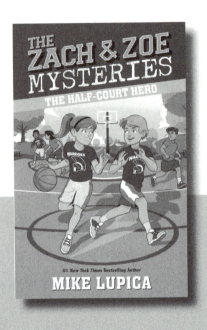

THE
ZACH & ZOE
MYSTERIES
THE HALF-COURT HERO

#1 *New York Times* Bestselling Author
MIKE LUPICA

When the twins start a summer basketball league at their local park, they notice the once run-down court is getting freshened up with each passing day. First new nets, then the benches have been completely restored. But who's behind it? Zach and Zoe are on the case!

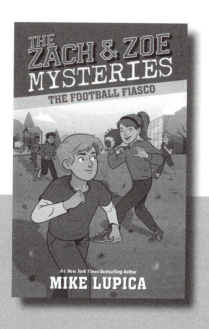

Zach and Zoe discover their recess football has been completely deflated, leaving them without a ball to play with. But who's behind it? By searching for clues around the school, Zach and Zoe uncover the truth behind the damaged ball, and learn the importance of friendship, inclusion, and being conscious of other people's feelings.

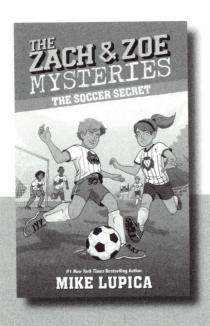

When a package arrives in the mail addressed
to Zach, the twins are surprised to find a soccer
jersey identical to the one Zach wears for his
team. But Zach's jersey is in his closet—so who
does this jersey belong to and why did they
send it? It's a soccer secret—and Zach and Zoe
are on the case!

THE ZACH & ZOE MYSTERIES
MYSTERIES
THE HOCKEY RINK HUNT

#1 New York Times Bestselling Author
MIKE LUPICA

When Zach and Zoe find out they'll be joining their dad at the Boston Bruins hockey practice, they can't believe their luck. But upon arrival, the Bruins' star player tells the twins he lost his lucky necklace right before the Stanley Cup final, and just like that, the mystery is on. The twins' search takes them all over the arena, and even onto the ice. Will Zach and Zoe find the missing necklace in time for the big game?

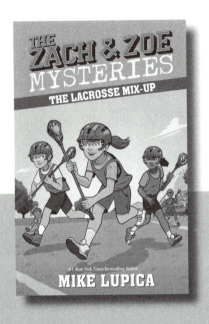

Zach and Zoe join the Middletown Elementary lacrosse club. But a day after their first game, a mystery presents itself: the netting on one of the school's lacrosse sticks is torn through. Ms. Moriarty says the equipment is just old and worn, but when the twins decide to investigate, they realize solving the mystery is only the first piece of an even bigger surprise.